The People's Republic of China

China is the world's oldest continuous civilization. The first Chinese dynasty took power about 1700 BC. By 221 BC, a strong central government was established; writing, currency, and weights and measures were standardized; the Great Wall was constructed. In 1912, the last emperor of China, a six-year-old boy named Pu Yi, stepped down, and a republic was proclaimed. In 1949, after a long civil war, Communist armies gained control of the Chinese mainland and established the People's Republic of China in Beijing. At the same time, opposing forces established a separate government, the Republic of China, on the island of Taiwan. Song Hai lives in the southeast of China, a region of prosperous farms that produce rice, tea, oranges, corn, and sweet potatoes. Other products include bamboo, silk, porcelain, lace, and carvings.

中国

Chinese Names

In China, a person's family name comes first and the given name second. When women marry, they keep their family name; children take the family name of their father. There are very few family names in China, and it is not unusual for there to be only four or five different ones in an entire village.

Chinese Writing and Language

People in China speak over 800 dialects of the Chinese language. These dialects are so different that a person from one part of the country usually cannot carry on a conversation with a person from another part. To ease this problem, the Chinese government has made the dialect spoken in the capital, Beijing, the official language used in schools and on television and radio. Now most people speak both their own dialect and the official "common language."

Chinese writing does not use an alphabet, but is made up of over 50,000 "characters," each one symbolizing a word or idea. The characters are not based on the way words sound, so even when Chinese people cannot understand each other's speech, they can read letters from each other! Because this system of writing is difficult to learn, the government has introduced a new system that uses the alphabet and is based on the pronunciation of the "common language."

Thank You, Meiling

Written by Linda Talley

Illustrated by Itoko Maeno

MarshMedia, Kansas City, Missouri

First Printing 1999
Second Printing 2000

Published by MARSH media
A Division of Marsh Film Enterprises, Inc.
P. O. Box 8082
Shawnee Mission, KS 66208

Library of Congress Cataloging-in-Publication Data
Talley, Linda.
Thank you, Meiling / written by Linda Talley; illustrated by Itoko Maeno.
p. cm.
Summary: An ill-mannered duck learns how to be courteous on a trip to the market with a Chinese boy who is buying mooncakes and lanterns to celebrate the Mid-autumn (Moon) Festival. Includes information about the phases of the moon, Chinese history and culture, and the Moon Festival.
ISBN 1-55942-118-5
[1. Mid-autumn Festival—Fiction. 2. Conduct of life—Fiction. 3. Ducks—Fiction. 4. China—Fiction.] I. Maeno, Itoko, ill. II. Title.
PZ7.T156355Th 1999 99-11853
[E]—dc21

Book layout and typography by Cirrus Design

Printed in Hong Kong

Special thanks to Maegan Branstetter — and to Poppy, Pansy, Rover, Cocoa, Babe, Daffy, and Sir Francis Drake.

They say this valley is like a dragon, its tail twined around the hills to the west, its head turned to the East China Sea. If that is so, then the village where I live is the dragon's eye.

When the sun comes up each morning, the eye of the dragon slowly opens. Shopkeepers throw wide their shutters. Housewives boil water for morning tea. Workers shuffle into their shoes for another day in the rice and tea fields. Our little flock stirs, impatient for our mistress to unfasten the latch on our pen.

Today she is slow, and I complain loudly.

"Hush, Meiling," my mother says. "Stop and think of others. Our mistress is busy in the kitchen, and the Old One is yet sleeping."

It is then that
the Old One slowly
makes his way out of the house
and into the courtyard. He is holding
a cup of tea in one hand, rubbing the sleep
from his eyes with the other. My mother looks at me
sternly, and our mistress scolds as she hurries to our pen.

Out we run, our webbed feet slapping on the cobblestones. Our mistress scoops rainwater from a wooden tub. We all run for the water pan, dip our heads in the cool water, and drink up.

"Meiling," calls my mother, "you've had your drink. Now make room for someone else." I hesitate, not wanting to give up my place around the small pan.

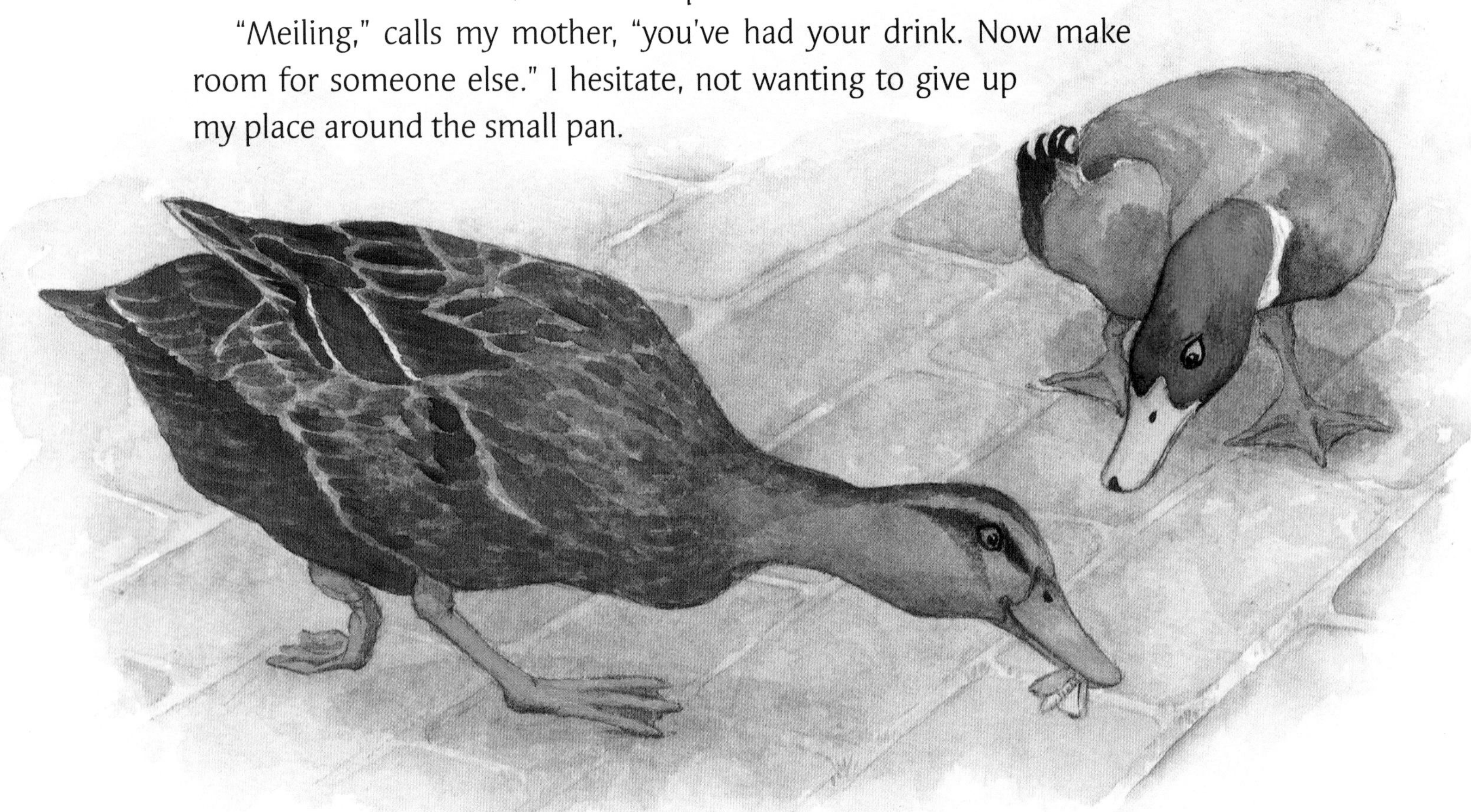

But then I see that my brother has spied a great moth and is chasing it around the courtyard. "Mine!" I quack loudly. I scurry in front of him and—SNAP—I've got it! Quickly I gulp it down.

"Meiling," my mother sighs, "do you think it is kind to—?"

"But it was mine!" I cry. "I saw it when I was drinking water and I chased it down and I caught it right in my bill and little brother would never have caught it—it would have flown away forever and nobody would have got it, not me or little brother or anyone else." I twitch my tail emphatically.

"Are you through, Meiling?" asks my mother. "You are not getting off to a good start this morning. You begin by being noisy and waking the Old One. You don't take turns at the water pan. You crowd in front of your brother to catch the moth. And now you interrupt me with your babbling."

At that moment a boy bursts from the doorway of our house. My mother's face brightens.

"I have an idea," she says. "Song Hai is running errands this morning. You shall go with him. If you pay attention, you may learn something about courtesy. Remember, stop and think of others."

That explains why, when Song Hai sets out from home, I am waddling down the lane behind him.

"Oh, so you are going with me today, are you, Meiling? Come along then," says Song Hai.

"These are very special errands," Song Hai explains. "Tomorrow is the day of the Moon Festival. Our first stop is the fruit vendor, and on this occasion we must buy only fruits that are round like the moon."

"Good morning, Mrs. Jiang," says Song Hai. "How are you? My mother asks if you would please select for me a small melon, three pomegranates, six peaches, a few crab apples, and a bunch of grapes."

Mrs. Jiang carefully packs the fruit into our basket. "Thank you very much, Mrs. Jiang!" says Song Hai.

"Good morning—please—thank you," I repeat to myself. "That's easy enough."

"Now we are going to buy something very special, just for me!" calls Song Hai.

I hurry behind him to a stall where paper lanterns of every shape and color dangle high overhead. "I know which one I want," says Song Hai. "The dragon lantern!"

Then we both hear it . . . tap . . . tap . . . tap.

Coming our way, cane in hand, is Mrs. Li, the oldest person in our village. Song Hai quickly sets down his basket and hurries to help her.

中秋節

Leaning on Song Hai's shoulder, Mrs. Li slowly makes her way to the lantern stall.

"Oh, I'm just in time. One last dragon lantern for my granddaughter," she says happily as she pays the vendor.

"Well, there are many other nice lanterns," sighs Song Hai. Then he laughs. "Look, Meiling! A lantern that looks like you!" When we leave the lantern stall, a duck-shaped lantern is swinging from Song Hai's shoulder.

"Help folks who can't get around very well," I tell myself, "even though it may mean a slight change of plans."

"Meiling," Song Hai says to me then, "let's rest in the shade of this tree, and I will tell you about the Moon Festival. Tomorrow is the fifteenth day of the eighth moon," he explains. "The moon will look bigger than at any other time of the year. Now is the time when we celebrate the good harvest and hear the old stories about the Rabbit in the Moon and the Moon Lady, Chang E."

While Song Hai is telling me about the Moon Festival, he unwraps a paper parcel. Inside is a bun sent by his mother for a snack. Just as he lifts it to his mouth, we hear a voice call out.

Song Hai's friend Go Ming runs to sit beside him. I see a wistful look flicker across Song Hai's face. He places his bun back on its wrapping, then tears it in half.

"Here, Go Ming," he says. "Please share my snack. It's too much for me to eat alone."

"Share treats with friends," I say to myself.

And that includes ducks I decide as I nibble bun crumbs that Song Hai and Go Ming toss my way.

"Next we must get mooncakes!" says Song Hai when we are again on our way. "A duck might not like these," he chuckles, "but I like them very much!" Away he runs, with me half running, half flying behind him.

Many people in our village are buying fat mooncakes this morning. "We shall have a little wait," frets Song Hai.

"Song Hai!" comes a voice from the front of the crowd. It is Song Hai's cousin, Song Ji-li. "Here!" she calls. "Get in front of me." Song Hai runs to the front of the line and slips in ahead of Song Ji-li.

"Hey, cousin," laughs Song Ji-li, "your duck is still at the end of the line."

Standing there, I feel confused. What am I to learn from this? "Stop and think of others," my mother has told me. As I stand there trying to sort it out, Song Hai looks at me. I look at Song Hai. I tap my webbed foot on the ground and let out three slow quacks, "Quack, quack, quack."

"Ji-li," says Song Hai, "I think my duck is trying to tell me something. And I think she's right. It won't be a long wait at the end of the line, and these other people have waited longer than I have."

And, in fact, it is not such a very long wait. Soon enough Song Hai has his own plump box of mooncakes.

There are other stops to make. We buy a bundle of rose flower incense, a Moon Palace poster, and a box of special tea for the Moon Festival celebration. It is lunchtime before we return home with our treasures.

The next evening the Moon Festival table is set up in our courtyard. On it are piled the melon, pomegranates, peaches, crab apples and grapes. Beside the fruit is a platter of beautiful mooncakes. The family sits outdoors, enjoying a special meal. Lanterns float overhead, lighting all the happy faces.

Later, as everyone sips tea and watches the full moon make its way high into the sky, the Old One tells stories about the Moon Palace and the people and animals who live there. An excited murmur goes up when at last the magical moment arrives . . .

. . . the moon above is mirrored in each teacup.

As a special treat, our mistress puts out a pan of chopped cucumbers. Hungry ducks soon surround the pan.

Then I notice my mother quietly watching us. I run back to her with a juicy chunk of cucumber.

"Mother," I cry, "I almost forgot my manners!"

"But you didn't," she says with a smile. "Thank you, Meiling!"

"You're welcome!" I quack, and then I hurry for my own Moon Festival treat.

Dear Parents and Educators:

Courteous people have the emotional maturity to curb impulsiveness and look beyond "me" to "we." They understand that courtesy helps prevent conflicts, demonstrates respect for the rights of others, and expresses sensitivity to those in need. Courtesy is necessary for the smooth functioning of society and the bonus is that you feel great about yourself, too! Considerate behavior, kind language, and generous compliments are day brighteners for everyone! Courteous people enjoy being civil to others, and they have found that their example encourages people around them to be more respectful and compassionate as well.

Encourage children to share their ideas and feelings about Meiling's experiences. Here are some questions to help initiate discussion about the message of *Thank You, Meiling*.

- How was Meiling treating the other ducks in the courtyard at the beginning of the story?
- Was she using good manners?
- What lessons did Meiling learn on her outing?
- Tell about a time when you used good manners. How did you feel?

As adults we marvel at children with good manners. We appreciate the maturity that they show and react to them in a warm and positive way. Their behavior did not just happen though! Caring adults helped these lucky youngsters develop their valuable interpersonal skills. Here are some ways that you can encourage courteous behavior in the children you live with or teach each day.

- Work to create a climate of gentle language, respect, and tolerance in your home or classroom.
- Teach and model specific skills, such as taking turns, making introductions, and answering the telephone.
- Teach and model sincere apologies and expect youngsters to use them when appropriate.
- Never minimize bad manners with excuses such as "He's tired" or "She's just angry."
- Discuss examples of courteous and discourteous behavior depicted on television or in movies.
- Celebrate courteous behaviors youngsters choose to use.

Available from MarshMedia

These storybooks, each hardcover with dust jacket and full-color illustrations throughout, are available at bookstores, or you may order by calling MarshMedia toll free at 1-800-821-3303.

Amazing Mallika, written by Jami Parkison, illustrated by Itoko Maeno. 32 pages. ISBN 1-55942-087-1.

Bailey's Birthday, written by Elizabeth Happy, illustrated by Andra Chase. 32 pages. ISBN 1-55942-059-6.

Bastet, written by Linda Talley, illustrated by Itoko Maeno. 32 pages. ISBN 1-55942-161-4.

Bea's Own Good, written by Linda Talley, illustrated by Andra Chase. 32 pages. ISBN 1-55942-092-8.

Clarissa, written by Carol Talley, illustrated by Itoko Maeno. 32 pages. ISBN 1-55942-014-6.

Emily Breaks Free, written by Linda Talley, illustrated by Andra Chase. 32 pages. ISBN 1-55942-155-X.

Feathers at Las Flores, written by Linda Talley, illustrated by Andra Chase. 32 pages. ISBN 1-55942-162-2.

Following Isabella, written by Linda Talley, illustrated by Andra Chase. 32 pages. ISBN 1-55942-163-0.

Gumbo Goes Downtown, written by Carol Talley, illustrated by Itoko Maeno. 32 pages. ISBN 1-55942-042-1.

Hana's Year, written by Carol Talley, illustrated by Itoko Maeno. 32 pages. ISBN 1-55942-034-0.

Inger's Promise, written by Jami Parkison, illustrated by Andra Chase. 32 pages. ISBN 1-55942-080-4.

Jackson's Plan, written by Linda Talley, illustrated by Andra Chase. 32 pages. ISBN 1-55942-104-5.

Jomo and Mata, written by Alyssa Chase, illustrated by Andra Chase. 32 pages. ISBN 1-55942-051-0.

Kiki and the Cuckoo, written by Elizabeth Happy, illustrated by Andra Chase. 32 pages. ISBN 1-55942-038-3.

Kylie's Concert, written by Patty Sheehan, illustrated by Itoko Maeno. 32 pages. ISBN 1-55942-046-4.

Kylie's Song, written by Patty Sheehan, illustrated by Itoko Maeno. 32 pages. (Advocacy Press) ISBN 0-911655-19-0.

Minou, written by Mindy Bingham, illustrated by Itoko Maeno. 64 pages. (Advocacy Press) ISBN 0-911655-36-0.

Molly's Magic, written by Penelope Colville Paine, illustrated by Itoko Maeno. 32 pages. ISBN 1-55942-068-5.

My Way Sally, written by Mindy Bingham and Penelope Paine, illustrated by Itoko Maeno. 48 pages. (Advocacy Press) ISBN 0-911655-27-1.

Papa Piccolo, written by Carol Talley, illustrated by Itoko Maeno. 32 pages. ISBN 1-55942-028-6.

Pequeña the Burro, written by Jami Parkison, illustrated by Itoko Maeno. 32 pages. ISBN 1-55942-055-3.

Plato's Journey, written by Linda Talley, illustrated by Itoko Maeno. 32 pages. ISBN 1-55942-100-2.

Tessa on Her Own, written by Alyssa Chase, illustrated by Itoko Maeno. 32 pages. ISBN 1-55942-064-2.

Thank You, Meiling, written by Linda Talley, illustrated by Itoko Maeno. 32 pages. ISBN 1-55942-118-5.

Time for Horatio, written by Penelope Paine, illustrated by Itoko Maeno. 48 pages. (Advocacy Press) ISBN 0-911655-33-6.

Toad in Town, written by Linda Talley, illustrated by Itoko Maeno. 32 pages. ISBN 1-55942-165-7.

Tonia the Tree, written by Sandy Stryker, illustrated by Itoko Maeno. 32 pages. (Advocacy Press) ISBN 0-911655-16-6.

Companion videos and activity guides, as well as multimedia kits for classroom use, are also available. MarshMedia has been publishing high-quality, award-winning learning materials for children since 1969. To order or to receive a free catalog, call 1-800-821-3303, or visit us at www.marshmedia.com.

Phases of the Moon

Our moon has no light of its own. The brightness we see is a reflection of the sun's light off the moon's surface. Half of the moon — the part facing the sun — is always shining with this reflected light. Because of the movement of the earth and the moon, our view of the illuminated portion of the moon changes from day to day. At times we can see only a sliver. At other times none at all! And at times we see a full shining circle, a full moon. It takes the moon about 29½ days to go from one full moon to the next.

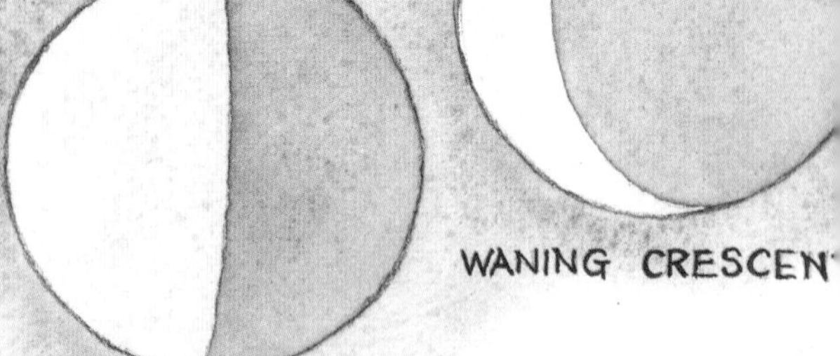

FULL MOON

FIRST QUARTER

WAXING CRESCENT

Moon Festival

The Chinese calendar is based in part on the phases of the moon. Each month has twenty-nine or thirty days, and the fifteenth day is always the day of the full moon. On the fifteenth day of the eighth lunar month (near the end of September on our calendar), people in China celebrate the Moon Festival, also called the Mid-autumn Festival. The harvests are in, and the full moon looks bigger than at any other time of the year. This a good night to sit outside and watch the moon rise while remembering old stories about the moon and its inhabitants.

Inhabitants of the Chinese Moon

In this country, we speak of the man in the moon. Chinese people see other images, including a lady and a rabbit. When the Moon Lady, Chang E, lived on earth, she swallowed a pill of immortality belonging to her husband. Immediately she found that she could fly! When Chang E heard her husband returning home, she feared he would be angry with her for taking the pill. She flew out the window and didn't stop flying until she came to the moon. Chang E still lives on the moon, where she rules from her Moon Palace. Another resident of the moon, the Moon Rabbit, spends his time pounding together ingredients to make a magic potion of immortality.

Mooncakes

For days before the Moon Festival, bakeries throughout China are bursting with mooncakes. Some are filled with fruits and nuts, others with duck eggs, pork and vegetables. Mooncakes are exchanged as gifts between friends and relatives, and on the night of the Moon Festival, a plate of thirteen cakes is often placed on the celebration table, one for each month in the lunar calendar.

月餅